To S. V. C., good friend then and now
F. P. H.

Text copyright © 1968 by Florence Parry Heide and Sylvia Van Clief
Illustrations copyright © 2003 by Holly Meade

First Candlewick Press edition 2003

Library of Congress Cataloging-in-Publication Data

Heide, Florence Parry.
That's what friends are for / Florence Parry Heide and Sylvia Van Clief ; illustrated by Holly
Meade. — 1st ed.
p.   cm.
Summary: All the elephant's friends give him advice, but none can solve his problem until the
opossum announces friends are to help, not just to give advice.
ISBN 0-7636-1397-5
[1. Elephants—Fiction. 2. Animals—Fiction. 3. Friendship—Fiction.]
I. Van Clief, Sylvia. II. Meade, Holly, ill. III. Title.
PZ7.H36 Tg 2003
[E]—dc21   00-057207

2 4 6 8 10 9 7 5 3 1

Printed in China

This book was typeset in Slimbach.
The illustrations were done in watercolor and cut paper collage.

Candlewick Press
2067 Massachusetts Avenue
Cambridge, Massachusetts 02140

visit us at www.candlewick.com

That's What Friends Are For

Florence Parry Heide and Sylvia Van Clief

illustrated by Holly Meade

CANDLEWICK PRESS
CAMBRIDGE, MASSACHUSETTS

Theodore the elephant
is sitting in the middle of the forest.
He has hurt his leg.

What a pity!
Today Theodore was going
to meet his cousin
at the end of the forest.

"What can I do?" Theodore says.
"My cousin is at the end of the forest,
and here I am in the middle of the forest.
And I have a bad leg, and I can't walk.

"I know what I'll do," Theodore says.
"I'll ask my friends for advice.
That's what friends are for."

Along comes Theodore's
friend the bird.

"Why are you sitting here
in the middle of the forest?"
asks the bird.

"Because I have a bad leg,
  and I can't walk.
  And I can't meet my cousin
  at the end of the forest," says Theodore.

"If *I* had a bad leg,
  I would fly to the end of the forest,"
  says the bird to Theodore.

"It's nice of you to give advice,"
  says Theodore to the bird.

"That's what friends are for,"
  says the bird.

Along comes Theodore's friend
the daddy longlegs.

"Why are you sitting here
in the middle of the forest?"
asks the daddy longlegs.

"Because I have a bad leg,
and I can't walk.
And I can't fly.
And I can't meet my cousin
at the end of the forest," says Theodore.

"If *I* had a bad leg,"
  says the daddy longlegs,
"I could walk anyhow—
  because I have seven other legs."

"It's nice of you to give advice,"
  says Theodore.

"That's what friends are for,"
  says the daddy longlegs.

Along comes Theodore's friend
the monkey.

"Why are you sitting here
in the middle of the forest?"
asks the monkey.

"Because I have a bad leg,
and I can't walk.
And I can't fly.
And I don't have seven other legs.
And I can't meet my cousin
at the end of the forest,"
says Theodore.

"If *I* had a bad leg," says the monkey,
"I would swing by my tail from the trees, like this."

"Well," says Theodore,
"I may have a very weak tail,
  but I have a very strong trunk."

Theodore grabs the
tree with his trunk . . .

Crash!

"Well, anyhow," says Theodore,
"thank you for your advice."

"That's what friends are for,"
says the monkey.

Along comes Theodore's friend the crab.

"Why are you lying down
in the middle of the forest?"
asks the crab.

"Because I have a bad leg,
and I can't walk.
And I can't fly.
And I don't have seven other legs.

"And I can't swing from the trees
by my tail (OR my trunk).
And I can't meet my cousin
at the end of the forest,"
says Theodore.

"If *I* had a bad leg," says the crab,
"I would get rid of it and grow another one."

"It's nice of you to give advice,"
  says Theodore.

"That's what friends are for,"
  says the crab.

Along comes Theodore's friend the lion.

"Why are you sitting here
in the middle of the forest?"
asks the lion.

"Because I have a bad leg,
 and I can't walk.
 And I can't fly.
 And I don't have seven other legs.
 And I can't swing from the trees
 by my tail (OR my trunk).
 And I can't grow another leg.
 And I can't meet my cousin
 at the end of the forest," says Theodore.

"If *I* had a bad leg," says the lion,
"I would roar so loud that
 everyone would come running
 to see what was the matter."

And he

roars.

"What's all the noise?"
    the opossum asks.
    He is hanging upside down by his tail.

"Theodore can't fly," says the bird.
"He can't get to the end of the forest
    to see his cousin," says the lion.
"We are giving him advice," says the crab.
"That's what friends are for."

"Nonsense," says the opossum.
"Friends are to *help*.
    Bring the cousin to Theodore."

So all the friends
go to find Theodore's cousin
at the end of the forest.

And they bring the cousin
to Theodore.

Theodore and his cousin
and all the friends are having a party.

"Thank you for *helping* me,"
says Theodore to his friends.

"That's what friends are for,"
say the friends.

To give advice is very nice,
but friends can do much more.
Friends should always help a friend.
That's what friends are for!